DOCTOR SMURF

Peyo

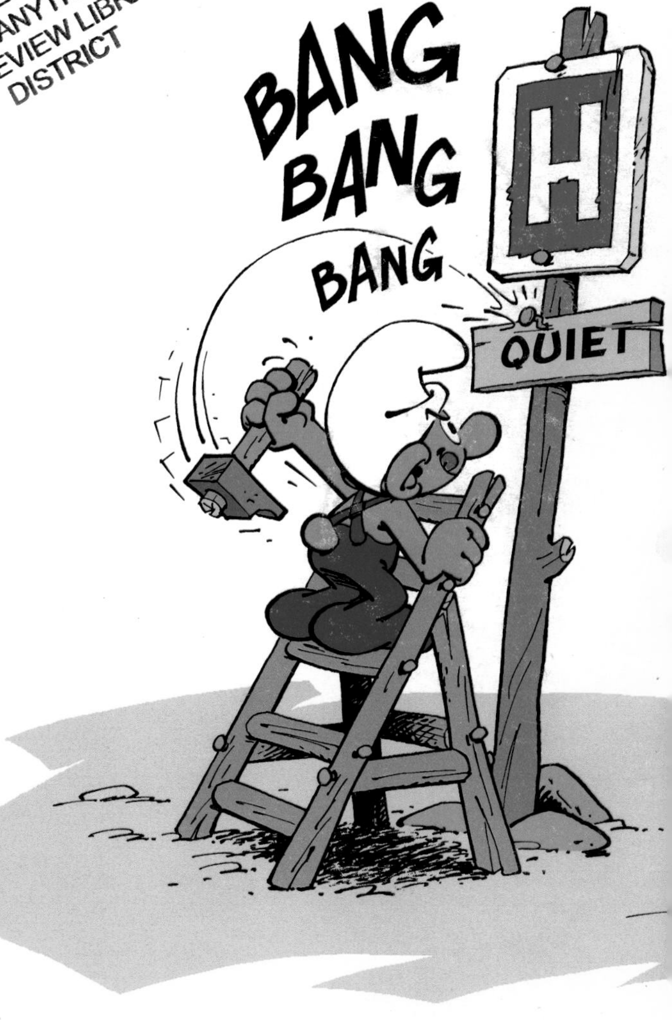
BANG
BANG
BANG
H
QUIET

DOCTOR SMURF

A SMURFS GRAPHIC NOVEL BY Peyo

WITH THE COLLABORATION OF
LUC PARTHOENS AND THIERRY CULLIFORD — SCRIPT
ALAIN MAURY AND LUC PARTHOENS — ARTWORK
NINE AND STUDIO LÉONARDO — COLOR

PAPERCUTZ™
NEW YORK

SMURFS GRAPHIC NOVELS AVAILABLE FROM PAPERCUTZ ™

THE SMURFS graphic novels are available in paperback for $5.99 each and in hardcover for $10.99 each at booksellers everywhere. You can also order online at papercutz.com. Or call 1-800-886-1223, Monday through Friday, 9 – 5 EST. MC, Visa, and AmEx accepted. To order by mail, please add $4.00 for postage and handling for first book ordered, $1.00 for each additional book and make check payable to NBM Publishing. Send to: Papercutz, 160 Broadway, Suite 700, East Wing, New York, NY 10038.

THE SMURFS graphic novels are also available digitally wherever e-books are sold.

PAPERCUTZ.COM

DOCTOR SMURF

© Peyo - 2016 - Licensed through Lafig Belgium - www.smurf.com

English translation copyright © 2016 by Papercutz.
All rights reserved.

"Doctor Smurf"
BY PEYO
WITH THE COLLABORATION OF
LUC PARTHOENS AND THIERRY CULLIFORD FOR THE SCRIPT,
ALAIN MAURY AND LUC PARTHOENS FOR ARTWORK,
NINE AND STUDIO LÉONARDO FOR COLORS.

Joe Johnson, SMURFLATIONS
Adam Grano, SMURFIC DESIGN
Janice Chiang, LETTERING SMURFETTE
Matt. Murray, SMURF CONSULTANT
Jeff Whitman, SMURF COORDINATOR
Bethany Bryan, ASSOCIATE SMURFETTE
Jim Salicrup, SMURF-IN-CHIEF

PAPERBACK EDITION ISBN: 978-1-62991-433-6
HARDCOVER EDITION ISBN: 978-1-62991-434-3

PRINTED IN CHINA JANUARY 2016 BY WKT CO. LTD.
3/F PHASE 1 LEADER INDUSTRIAL CENTRE
188 TEXACO ROAD, TSEUN WAN, N.T., HONG KONG

Papercutz books may be purchased for business or promotional use. For information on bulk purchases please contact Macmillan Corporate and Premium Sales Department at (800) 221-7945 x5442.

DISTRIBUTED BY MACMILLAN
FIRST PAPERCUTZ PRINTING

Golly, wanting to fix my fence was really smurfy of you!

The pleasure is ours, Farmer Smurf! Look out, Clumsy Smurf, smurf tight and, above all, don't move!

THUMP

Uh... I'm sorry, Clumsy Smurf!...

PAPA SMURF! Papa Smurf! Come quick!

?

A few seconds later...

Hey, I didn't move, did I?

Uh... No, no, Clumsy Smurf! That was very good!

Okay, this isn't serious! With this poultice, he'll be on his two smurfs again tomorrow. Next time, you both pay better attention!

It's lucky Papa Smurf is here! What would we smurf without him?

Yep! Sure enough!

Thanks to him, we're never sick, and we can smurf without worry!

Sure enough!

1

One morning, however...

Oooo, my smurf hurts this morning!

I look like Grouchy Smurf... And my blue is so pale!

And my hanging tongue! For smurf's sake, I'm catching something! I'd better go see Papa Smurf!

Two drops of hellebore extract--

NOK NOK NOK

?!

What is it? I'd asked not to be disturbed during this experiment!

I know, Papa Schmurf, but ish important! I'm shick!

AGAIN! Well then! What's wrong with you this time?

Thish morning, my head wath schmurfing like the brath band'th big drum, and I had a shtabbing thenthathion here!

GRUMMBL

Okay, come in, I'll examine you! Let's see that thermomesmurf!

And a few moments later...

So, you're sure, Papa Smurf? It's nothing serious?

Absolutely! You have no reason to smurf yourself! Some vegetable broth, a little rest, and tomorrow you'll feel like a new Smurf!

For smurf's sake! And knowing it's all smurfing in his head! Interesting as a case of psychosomasmurf! One day, I'll have to smurf on his case.

Laboratory

?

2

Hello, Smurf! What's going on? You don't look so smurf!

Oh, no!

I'm returning from a visit to Papa Smurf, because I'm very, very sick, and he told me to smurf a vegetable broth!

Vegetable broth? That's all? That seems a little paltry to me!

To me, too!

SCRTCH SCRTCH

Why don't you smurf a horehound infusion?

A horehound infusion!? You think?

Absolutely! It's a root, it seems. In any case, that's what Farmer Smurf said to me!

Or was it Chef Smurf? I don't remember!

In any case, if it doesn't smurf you any good, it can't smurf you any harm!

You're right. That seems like a more serious cure to me! I'll go try it right away!

The next day...

Hey! Smurf! Hey!

?

Your cure was truly a miracle! My symptoms from yesterday have disappeared!

You see, I'd smurfed you so!

?

On the other hand, my throat is as dry as a wooden smurf and, since this mornving, when I smurf the slightest effort, I get dizzy!

3

In my opinion, for your throat, you must smurf an infusion of horehound! As for the dizziness, I think a concoction of blackberry bush roots would be appropriate!

Come on, Sneezy Smurf, Papa Smurf has already smurfed you a hundred times there's nothing wrong with you! All this fuss is a lot of smurf!

?

!

Smurf him alone, Handy Smurf! This Smurf really needs someone to look after his health!

Furthermore haven't you yourself ever complained of back pains after smurfing in your workshop for several days? Or having your head feeling like a melon after smurfing over a plan all night long?

?!

Uh... Yes, but...

You see?! In your place, I'd smurf on my guard! Maybe you're sick, but you don't have time to realize it!

♪Pff!♪ What you're saying is stupid!

That smurf is crazy!

Those words, however, had sown doubt in Handy Smurf's mind...

BANG BANG

And the next day...

And above all, don't forget to let the blackberry bush roots smurf in an infusion of sarsaparilla for two hours. It's important!

4

Um!

?

Handy Smurf? What are you smurfing there?

Uh... I'd like to smurf to you about something or other... ¿Hmm¿... in private!

Come in then! We'll smurf more peacefully inside!

Thanks!

I'm all ears, Handy Smurf.

So here goes. I smurfed about what you said to me yesterday and...

And you didn't smurf a wink last night!

Uh... Yes, in fact!

And of course, today, you're tired, unenergetic, and the only thing you want to do is to smurf in your bed!

How did you know?

It's typical, my dear friend! You're smurfing from anxiety due to overwork, and that's keeping you from smurfing at night!

Is it serious?

No, but you must smurf a treatment immediately! First, no more work. Next, you'll smurf an elixir of hawthorn extract!

Don't worry! I'll smurf all this down for you!

5

SCRITCH SCRATCH

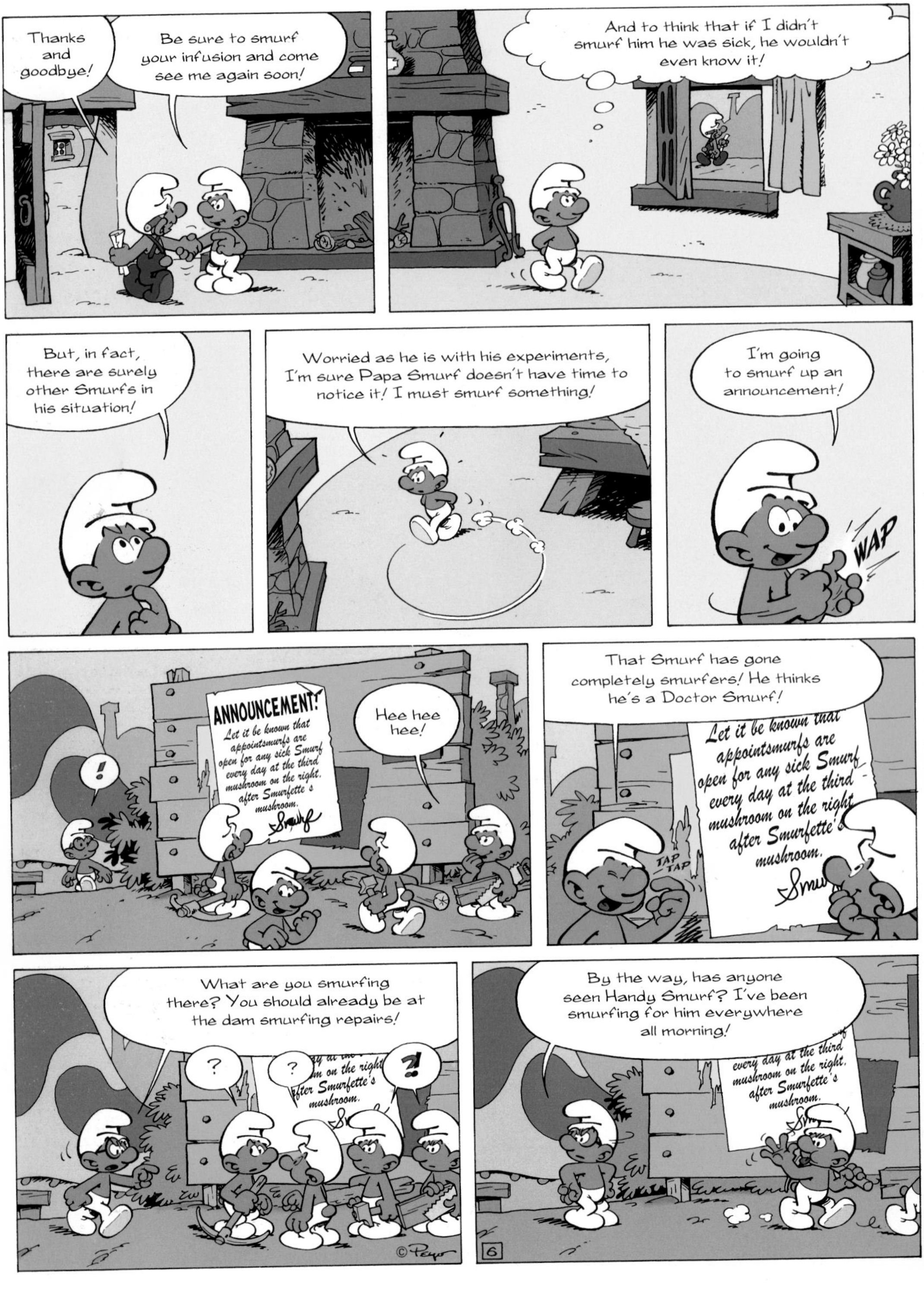
Thanks and goodbye!
Be sure to smurf your infusion and come see me again soon!
And to think that if I didn't smurf him he was sick, he wouldn't even know it!
But, in fact, there are surely other Smurfs in his situation!
Worried as he is with his experiments, I'm sure Papa Smurf doesn't have time to notice it! I must smurf something!
I'm going to smurf up an announcement!
WAP
ANNOUNCEMENT!
Let it be known that appointsmurfs are open for any sick Smurf every day at the third mushroom on the right, after Smurfette's mushroom.
!
Hee hee hee!
That Smurf has gone completely smurfers! He thinks he's a Doctor Smurf!
TAP TAP
What are you smurfing there? You should already be at the dam smurfing repairs!
?
?
?!
© Peyo
By the way, has anyone seen Handy Smurf? I've been smurfing for him everywhere all morning!
6

Meanwhile...

And there's the final touch!

BAM BAM

DOCTOR'S OFFICE

I'm impatient to see my future patients in my office!

A
SEI
GRCX
YTUYPA

Later, however...

TAP TAP
TAP TAP

And much, much later...

For Smurf's sake! Not a single visit all day long! Do they distrust me?

The reckless fools! With all the illnesses smurfing around nowadays, they don't know what they're smurfing!

I absolutely must smurf up with a way so they'll come to my office!

Hello, Smurf!

Hello, Smurfette!

DOCTOR'S OFFICE

Uh, Smurfette! Could you give me a few moments?

Unless... Why of course! Why didn't I smurf of that earlier?

The next day, at the village square...

HEAR YE, HEAR YE! AN ANNOUNCEMENT FOR THE POPULASMURF!

RAM BANG GLONG

7

11

We remind you that the new doctor's been available for appointsmurfs since yesterday. Just because you think you're in good shape that doesn't mean you're not sick. From now on, you're smurfily advised to smurf yourself to the office smurfs if you don't want to become sick for real!

BAH! That crazy smurf again!

HEH HEH

You are further advised that Smurfette has kindly accepted to smurf herself to the service to the Smurfs' health!

And that she will be in charge of welcoming every new patient in a waiting room smurfed for that purpose!

ZOOM

ZOOM

! ?

Well, anyway, I have to go smurf that potion that Dr. Smurf prescribed for me!

No, sir, no! I was before you!

No way!

Let me smurf ahead! I'm very, very sick!

What are they giving out?

Chestnuts!

I don't know what's going on, but since there was a line, I smurfed into it!

?

So, Greedy Smurf? To what do I owe the pleasure?

Well... SCRUNCH... It was for Smurfette!

© Peyo

Hmm, tell me! How many of those cookies do you smurf per day?

?

8

I don't know! A carton or two! They're smurfily good!

Wouldn't that be three or four instead?

Uh, maybe!

And your smurf never aches?

No!

But if I smurf there with my wand!? Don't you feel something?

OOF!

I thought so! Look at your weight! You smurf at least one ounce too much!

Really?

Greedy Smurf, if you go on like this, you'll soon be nothing more than a big, fat smurf, and you'll be the laughingstock of all the Smurfs!

HEE HEE HEE!

Huh!?... What must I smurf?

Smurf my advice!

Smurfette, smurf in the next patient!

So, Greedy Smurf! How was it?

No more cookies, a few orange seeds for every meal, and never smurfing between meals! Smurfing that to me!

WAP WAP

Sit there and breathe in deep, Jokey Smurf! I'm going to smurf your heart!

Hmm, that all seems perfectly smurf! The beat is regular!

Pfff....

TIC TOC TIC TOC

BANG!

I'll prescribe cod liver oil to smurf every time before smurfing a trick! Maybe that will make you think twice!

By the way, I smurfed a little gift for you!

You shouldn't have!

TIC TOC TIC TOC

NEXT!

KABLAM

Obviously, that Jokey Smurf is a hopeless case!

?

Um, I see what's wrong!

Aaaaaaaaah! The Smurfette!

Tonight, before you go to bed, smurf two drops of this potion! If you don't smurf better by tomorrow, medicine can't do anything for you!

Next!

Meanwhile, in the laboratory...

No, it's no use! It's not smurfing! I must surely be missing an important ingredient!

I'm too smurfed to go on... I'll go rest for a little bit...

ATCHOO!

?

KLIK KLAK

Well, well, Vanity Smurf?! You don't look so good! Have you smurfed a cold?

SNIF

Don't worry, Papa Smurf! The Doctor Smurf gave—m–M–M—

ATCHOO!

Sorry! He prescribed me a potion to smurf before every meal!

SNIF

Doctor Smurf, you say? What is all this smurfiness? And he prescribed this for you? But this is ridiculous!

PAPA SMURF! I finally smurfed the saltpeter you asked me for!

?

© Peyo [11]

Saltpeter?! Why of course! It had completely smurfed out of my head! That's the missing ingredient! Thanks, Miner Smurf!

Vanity Smurf, do me the favor of smurfing this prescription in the wastebasket and smurfing a nice herbal tea with honey before smurfing to bed!

And despite his fatigue, Papa Smurf resumed his experiments...

Okay let's resmurf everything from the top!

As for Vanity Smurf, he soon reported Papa Smurf's words to Dr. Smurf...

Herbal tea... HA! HA! HA!

With all respect due to him, Papa Smurf practices a very old-fashioned sort of medicine!

Believe me, smurf my recommendations to the letter, and everything will be fine!

Tomorrow, I'll smurf you a little visit to see if all is well!

Thanks, Doctor, that reassures me!

Hey, that makes me think I should smurf a little visit to Handy Smurf!

Smurfette, I'm going out! Resmurf all my appointments till tomorrow!

Yes, doctor!

That Doctor Smurf seems like he's smurfing a rather revolutionary kind of medicine!

12

At Handy Smurf's...

Everything seems fine to me! You can smurf your overalls back on.

YAWN! It's funny how I want to sleep every time I smurf your potion!

?

Want to sleep? Every time after drinking this potion? Really?

RRRrr ZZ ZZz

?

It's incredible! I've just smurfed a new sleeping aid! That's the proof I was made to be a doctor!

Soon, Doctor Smurf's popularity would grow in a spectacular fashion.

13

17

?

Z

Lazy Smurf! Malingsmurfing again!

ZZZ

Go on! Get to smurf like everyone else, because like Papa Smurf always says, "Idleness is the root of all smurfs and...

For smurf's sake! Smurfing! Always smurfing! It's enough to make you sick!

Hey! That smurfs me an idea!

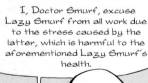

A smurfily good idea, too! Hee hee!

You were right to come see me, Lazy Smurf! I'll smurf you a medical excuse!

Thanks, Doctor!

I, Doctor Smurf, excuse Lazy Smurf from all work due to the stress caused by the latter, which is harmful to the aforementioned Lazy Smurf's health.

"...excused from all work due to the stress caused by the latter..."! HA! HA! HA! Hey, did the rest of you smurf that?!

14

But...but?! What are you smurfing?

Stop!

Where are you going?

Excuse us, Brainy Smurf, but we have an important meeting with Doctor Smurf!

They've all smurfed out of their minds!

You also want me to smurf you an excuse? Obviously it's an epidemic!

I was here before him, Smurfette!

That's not true!

Come, come! Calmly smurf your turn, and no arguing!

It's a catasmurfre! There's not a single Smurf at the construction site now!

Do I count for a smurf?

Ahh! This is not how it's going to smurf! I'll go smurf Papa Smurf!

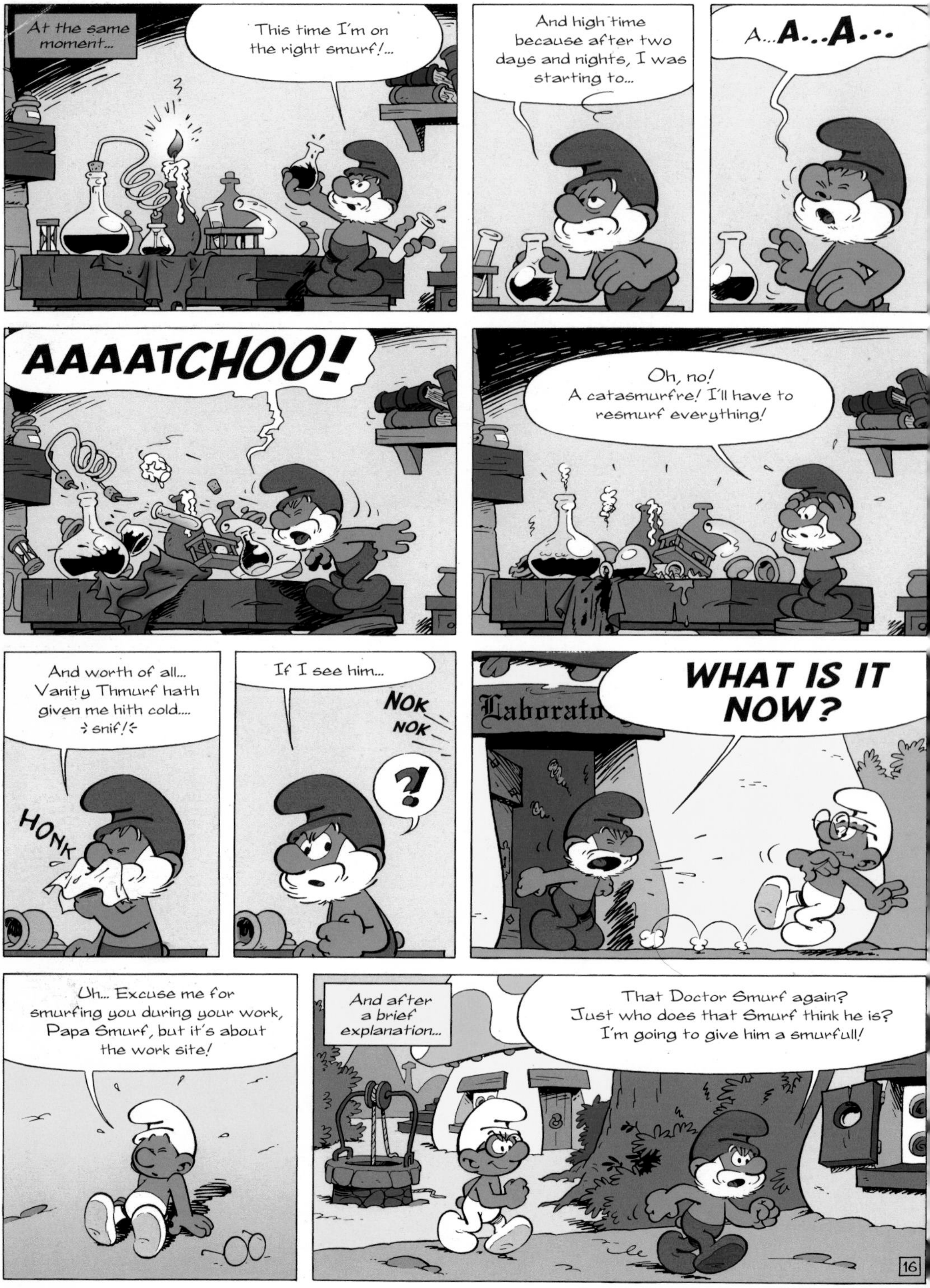
At the same moment...
This time I'm on the right smurf!...
And high time because after two days and nights, I was starting to...
A...A...A...
AAAATCHOO!
Oh, no! A catasmurfre! I'll have to resmurf everything!
And worth of all... Vanity Thmurf hath given me hith cold.... ⁞snif!⁞
HONK
If I see him...
NOK NOK
?!
Laborato
WHAT IS IT NOW?
Uh... Excuse me for smurfing you during your work, Papa Smurf, but it's about the work site!
And after a brief explanation...
That Doctor Smurf again? Just who does that Smurf think he is? I'm going to give him a smurfull!
16

At Doctor Smurf's...

Uh...are you sure it's really necessary for me to smurf my pants, Doctor?

Yes, Dopey Smurf!

?

Who could be smurfing all that racket?

Well, Smurfette! What's...

...smurfing?

Uh, hello, Papa Smurf!

Ah! There you are!

WELL? It seems you're smurfing medicine in my place? And that you're smurfing disorder in the village?

B--but Papa Smurf, it was to help the Smurfs!

That's right, Papa Smurf! Since he's been smurfing medicine, none of us has smurfed sick!

And also, it seems he's smurfing a revolutionary kind of medicine!

ENOUGH! I don't want to know anything!

That's when the accumulated fatigue and the cold overcame Papa Smurf's anger...

?

I... I...

?

?

Heavens! Papa Smurf!

Look out! Grab him! He's going to fall!

No... I... Let me go!

OUCH

He's delirious! Smurf after him, I'll be right back!

Blazing stethoscopes! I was certain I'd smurfed it in my satchel!

Uh... Doctor!

Not now, Dopey Smurf! Now now!

Ah, there it is! Open his mouth, I'll smurf him my elixir of hawthorn extract.

I...No.. *GLUG GLUG*!

Smurf him into his bed! He needs lots of rest!

Don't worry, Smurfette! Thanks to my elixir, he'll be as fresh as a young Smurf in a few days!

Poor Papa Smurf!

18

Uh... Doctor?

Yes, what is it now, Dopey Smurf?

Excuse me, but it was just to smurf you if I could get dressed now?

?!

And the consultations resume with greater frequency...

That's too bad! You have to be careful when you're smurfing a fence.

Well, it's because he was too busy laughing at one of Jokey Smurf's smurfs!

It's okay, Smurf! I'm here!

WOOOO AHHHH!

Don't cry! I'll smurf you a little bandage and it'll be all better!

So then, I'll smurf the bandage here and wrap it around your hand...

I'll resmurf it this way... I'll pass it underneath!

SNIP SNIP

I'll smurf a little knot!

Another!

I'll cut!

?

And there you go!

?

?

?

Hello? What's that smurf sticking out there?

?

POKE

OUCH MY FINGER!

19

23

Yes... Uh... Smurf him to my office. Smurfette will finish the bandage!

What a smurf that Doctor Smurf is! He's smurfing such a revolutionary medicine, I don't understand anything about it!

Doctor Smurf's renown has now spread throughout the village...

Or almost...

Oh! Hello! How's it smurfing?

It's smurfing. And you?

It's smurfing all right! Are you coming back from a appointsmurf at Doctor Smurf's?

Yes, he smurfed me three potions to take after every meal.

Only three? He smurfed me five!

Five potions!? Whoa! That's serious!

?!

Me, I don't like Doctor Smurf and his potions!

Oh, Grouchy Smurf, you never like anything or anyone!

What's more, he told me that, if I smurfed his potions, I wouldn't get sick! He was right, because I'm not!

So there!

Me, I don't like Smurfs who smurf potions to not be sick, when they aren't!

Unfortunately, this enthusiasm is not with its inconveniences...

What's wrong, Doctor? You look very preoccupied this morning!

Smurfette, this can't smurf on like this!

Between the visits I must smurf to Papa Smurf, Harmony Smurf, Vanity Smurf, and Poet Smurf...

As well as Lazy Smurf and Chef Smurf, it's very simple, I no longer have time to smurf my appointsmurfs!

Clearly, you wouldn't have this problem if you smurfed all you patients in the same place!

Why that **IS** clear! That's a marvelous idea, Smurfette! We're going to have a hospital smurfed!

POW

A little later, at Handy Smurf's...

Smurf a hospital! But that's impossible, Doctor! Thanks to you, all the Smurfs have a note not to work anymore!

Darn it! That's annoying!

?

Why, yes! Of course!

!

Let's smurf it in your workshop then!

?!

© Peyo 21

A little rearranging, a few smurfs of paint here and there, and it'll be perfect!

But... But?

Come on, Handy Smurf... You know full well it's the Smurfs' health!

Okay...

No sooner said than done...and the next day...

Look, Handy Smurf. Isn't our hospital smurfily beautiful?

EMERGENCY

H

QUIET

And there's our marvelous nurse already at work! Hello, Smurfette! How's it smurfing this morning?

Smurfette! Look after me! I'm very sick!

I'm sicker than he is, Smurfette!

That's not true! I am!

:Mmpff:..

Smurfette! The basin! QUICK!

Oops! Too late!

© Peyo 22

Ah, that Smurfette! I wonder what I'd smurf without her!

Shh! Here's Papa Smurf's bed! We smurfed him a little apart so it'd be more peaceful!

Okay, Papa Smurf! You have to smurf your potion!

:Mmpff:... :GLUG! GLUG!:

Meanwhile...

Look out! He's going to smurf!

Go on! Smurf!

I'm going to smurf him one of these potatoes through the goal!

?!

WOOAAAH!

Come on! Don't smurf like that! You missed your shot, it's no big deal!

:WHINE!:

A bit later...

?

Doctor, quick! There's a Smurf who broke his smurf while smurfing the ball!

23

© Peyo

That's a totally smurfect job for my new emergency service!

Quick! Get smurfing! There's an injured Smurf at the ball field! And remember nothing must smurf the ambulance!

CLAP CLAP

WOO! WOO! Go! You heard the doctor! Get smurfing, you slackers!

DING DING DING

♪

LOOK OUT! Let the ambulance smurf!

HEY!

DING DING DING DING

TCHOK

Such a nice day, isn't it? Ideal for smurfing your errands!

Yes, since our streets are safe nowadays!

DING DING DING

?

24

28

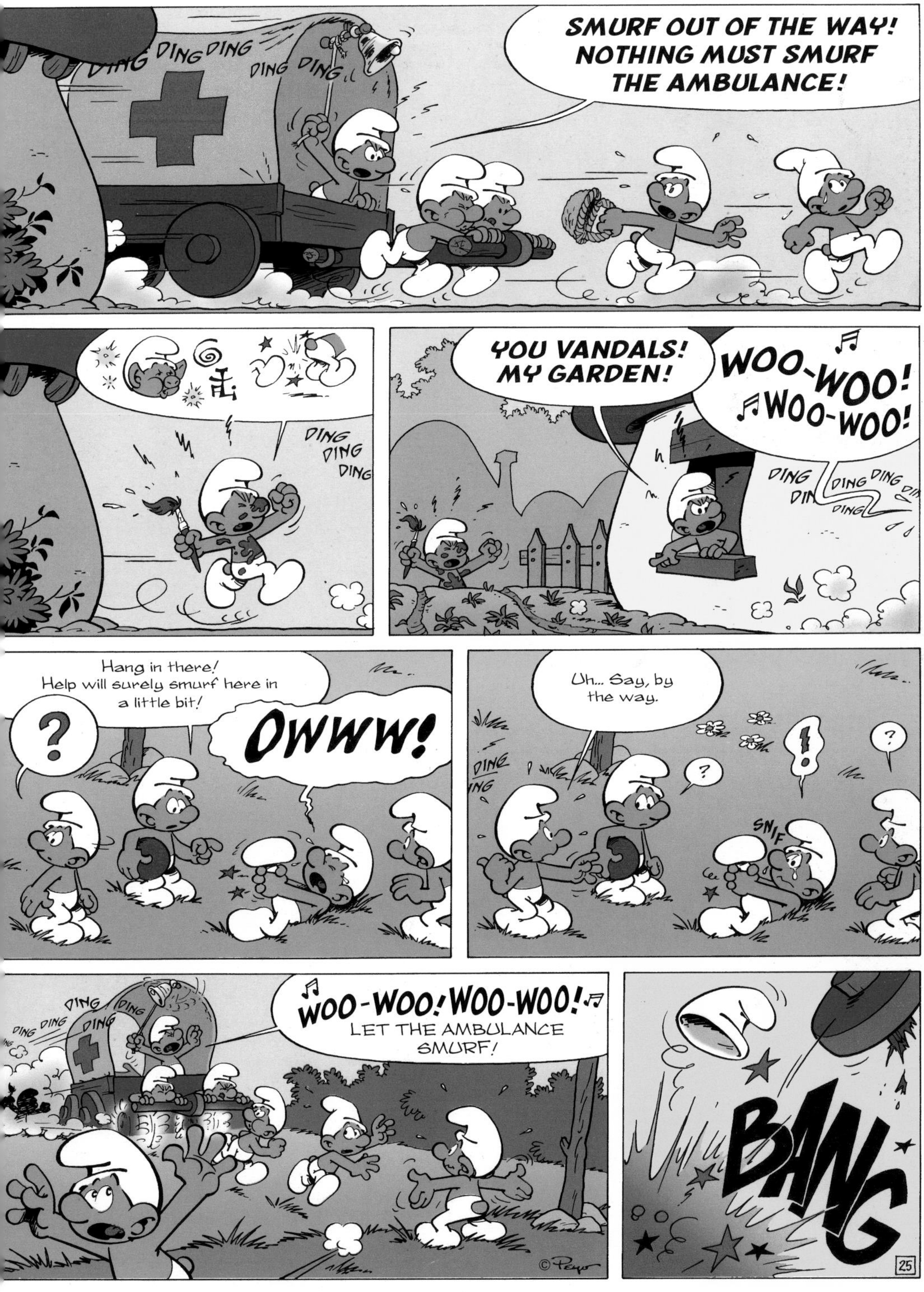
DING DING DING
DING DING
SMURF OUT OF THE WAY! NOTHING MUST SMURF THE AMBULANCE!
DING DING DING
YOU VANDALS! MY GARDEN!
WOO-WOO! WOO-WOO!
DING DING DING DING DING
Hang in there! Help will surely smurf here in a little bit!
?
OWWW!
DING
Uh... Say, by the way.
?
?
!
SNIF
DING DING DING DING
WOO-WOO! WOO-WOO!
LET THE AMBULANCE SMURF!
© Peyo
BANG
25

Uh...Doctor, the ambulance is back!

AH! FINALLY!

?

♪ WOO-WOO! ♪

?

ASSASSINS! BARSMURFIANS! MURDERERS! SMURFKILLERS!

DING DING DING

Doctor! There's another injured one! And it looks smurfily serious!

!?

Smurf him in the operating room. We'll smurf his leg!

♭ **AAAAH!**

?

!?

?

NO! For pity's sake! Don't smurf off my leg! **HELP ME, MY FRIENDS!**

Uh... I was just smurfing a few tools to put them away!

TAP TAP

26

Little by little, life in the village has deteriorated, and the village itself is left in a state of neglect...

It's impossible! It's impossible!

WOO WOO

DING DING

DING

THE WORST, HOWEVER, IS YET TO COME!...

Doctor! If you please!...

?

How's it smurfing, dear friend?

You see, at night, once I've eaten dinner, sometimes I smurf a kind of itch here! It smurfs or rather it tickles!

Careful! Let's not missmurf ourselves! Does it smurf you or does it tickle you?

Well, it tickles me! But it smurfs me a little, too.

SCRATCH SCRATCH SCRITCH

Doesn't it tickle more when you've smurfed a sarsaparilla gratin?

I never smurf any! But it does seem to me that if I smurfed some, in fact, it would tickle me more!

It's not very serious! I'll tell Smurfette to smurf you a little potion and everything will resmurf to normal!

27

SCRITCH SCRATCH

A little potion! A little potion! I'm already smurfing lots of little potions, and that's not stopping the tickling!

You're right. I'm fed up with Doctor Smurf, too! I'm sure Papa Smurf would smurf us other medicine!

Let's go smurf his opinion!

Good idea!

You wouldn't smurf us all these potions, would you, Papa Smurf?!

Give us some advice! What must we smurf to treat ourselves?

?

What are you smurfing here? Can't you see he's sick? Leave him alone and smurf back to your beds!

? ?

Come now, Papa Smurf! It's time for your potion! The doctor said to you must smurf it in order to rest!

NO! Biff?... It's no good!

We won't smurf anything! Let's go to his laboratory. Maybe we'll smurf something interesting there!

Good idea!

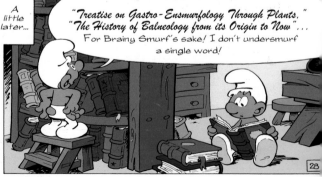

A little later...

"Treatise on Gastro-Ensmurfology Through Plants," "The History of Balneology from its Origin to Now"... For Brainy Smurf's sake! I don't undersmurf a single word!

28

I think I've smurfed something!

Show me!

It says here that certain illnesses are smurfed by people themselves who think they're sick. They call it psychosomasmurf illnesses.

I remember Papa Smurf always saying to Sneezy Smurf that it was all in his smurf.

And here, look! Acupuncsmurf! It's an old medicine smurfed in a very distant country by smurfing needles into your body...

Hee hee! That looks smurfily funny to me!

Funny, sure! But I think it'd be more serious to smurf illnesses in your head!

Well, I think it'd be better to smurf acupuncsmurf!

No way! That's smurfily stupid!

You're the one who's stupid!

OH, YEAH?

YEAH!

WHAT ARE YOU SMURFING HERE?

?!

You know full well it's forbidden to smurf into Papa Smurf's laboratory in his absence!

Go on! Out!

I'll prove I'm right!

We'll see about that!

Laboratory

KLIK KLAK

Don't think you'll smurf away with this, because I'll tell Papa Smurf...

!

Tell me, Brainy Smurf, it's a real sickness with you smurfing your finger like that while smurfing everybody...

?

In my opinion, all that must smurf in your head! Come see me in my future office, one of these smurfs!

?

?!?

And so each of them try out their new medicine...

I promise you this is a tested method, Vanity Smurf! You have nothing to smurf!

OWWWWW!

?

?

Come back! I haven't finished!

LOOK OUT, VANITY SMURF!

OWWWW!

30

OWWOWWOWWOUCH!

For smurf's sake, Vanity Smurf! Can't you watch where you're smurfing? You've smurfed all my cactuses!

Cactus spines? That's not a bad idea!

HURTS!

Elsewhere...

You see, Dopey Smurf, psychosmurfy says that all these problems smurf in our heads!

TAP TAP

You see, you for example, if you're so stupid it's because, when you were just a baby, everyone made smurf of you and called you Dopey Smurf!

...

What's more, I remember that when I'd smurf in the sandbox, they'd make smurf of me!

?

All because I didn't have a smurf like the others! Stupid sandbox! ⇗WAAAHH!⇖

BOOHOO HOO!

?

⇒SNIFF⇐... But now I'm a big Smurf and that's all in the past!...

SNIF

Thanks, Dopey Smurf! That really did me good to smurf with you about it! Thank you so much!

?!

What a marvelous sort of medicine! I feel smurfily better after this session!

? ? ? ? ?

SCRTCH SCRTCH

©Peyo 31

Others besides me are smurfing medicine? Why that's completely forbidden!

Of course, Doctor Smurf is soon informed of these initiatives...

WHAT?

EMERGENCIES

We'll see about that! Have them sent to my office!

Soon after...

I've been told you're smurfing medicine, too! Do you know you don't have the right to?!

And why not?

That's right! Why not?

Because I'm the only one authorized to be able to smurf it!

Why's that?

Right! Why's that?

Because of my diploma of "Doctor of Medicine" smurfed by the Academy of Smurfic Medicine!

Oh?

That's right! Oh?

32

© Peyo

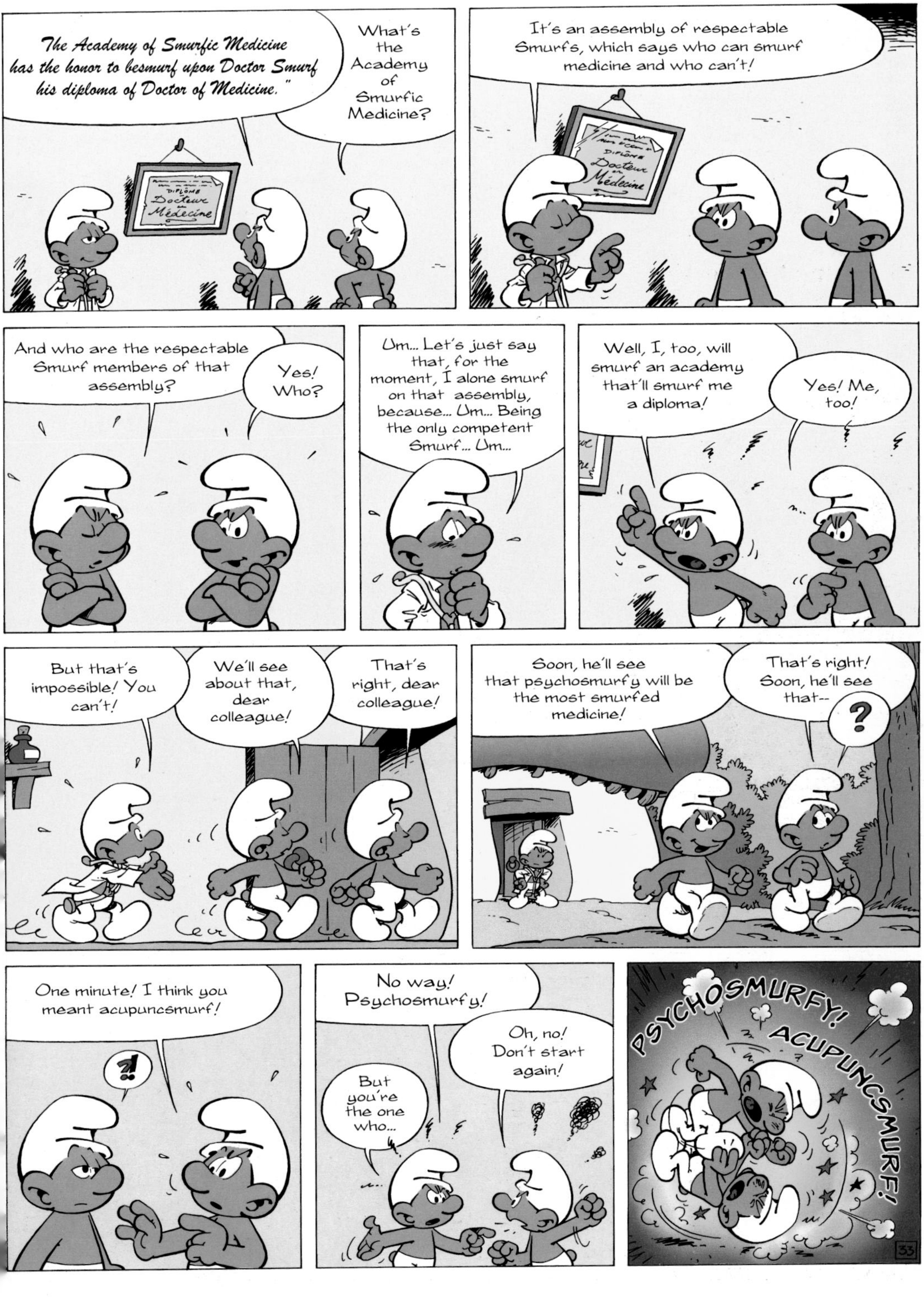
The Academy of Smurfic Medicine has the honor to besmurf upon Doctor Smurf his diploma of Doctor of Medicine."
What's the Academy of Smurfic Medicine?
It's an assembly of respectable Smurfs, which says who can smurf medicine and who can't!
And who are the respectable Smurf members of that assembly?
Yes! Who?
Um... Let's just say that, for the moment, I alone smurf on that assembly, because... Um... Being the only competent Smurf... Um...
Well, I, too, will smurf an academy that'll smurf me a diploma!
Yes! Me, too!
But that's impossible! You can't!
We'll see about that, dear colleague!
That's right, dear colleague!
Soon, he'll see that psychosmurfy will be the most smurfed medicine!
That's right! Soon, he'll see that--
?
One minute! I think you meant acupuncsmurf!
?!
No way! Psychosmurfy!
Oh, no! Don't start again!
But you're the one who...
PSYCHOSMURFY!
ACUPUNCSMURF!
33

And while at the hospital, Smurfette continues to devote herself body and soul...

¿Pfff¿, at this pace, I can't smurf on very much longer!

... The practice of the new medicines spreads in the village.

You'll see, Harmony Smurf! Thanks to acupuncsmurf, all your problems with bad notes will smurf away like magic!

I don't understand! I'll never be able to smurf the trumpet with these needles!

That's just what I meant!

?

SLAM

And when you were still only a baby Smurf, in the sandbox, didn't you already smurf yourself for an ambulance?

WOO-WOO-WOO-WOO.

Each type of medicine now has its supporters...

You should smurf away with all those potions! They're no good for you!

Acupuncsmurf! Psychosmurfy! These new disciplines don't insmurf me with any confidence! I prefer to smurf Doctor Smurf's potions! That's something concrete, at least!

Maybe, nevertheless, it's no thanks to him that we no longer have to smurf Harmony Smurf's wrong notes!

I assure you, thanks to psychosmurfy, I've become as strong as Hefty Smurf!

All this fuss makes me sick... And me, I don't like being sick!

© Peyo

34

That's right! Why couldn't I smurf medicine, too?

The craziest ideas give rise to as many new "new medicines":

Hydrosmurfapy...

?

Physiotherasmurf...

You must suffer if you want to get better!

OWW! OUCH!

Chiropodsmurfy, etc....

?

HEE HEE! HA! HA! HA!

Stop! Hee hee! It's too much!

HA! HA!

Certain Smurfs dedicate themselves to several medicines...

Uh oh! I'm late for my acupuncsmurf session! Quick, my potions! GLUG! GLUG!

And now, to the spa!

This way, at least, I'm sure to not smurf any illnesses!

And one day, the real drama arrives...

Come now, Papa Smurf! Don't be childish! The Doctor has said that--

That medicine smurfs no effect of me, Smurfette! And you know as well as I do Doctor Smurf isn't a real doctor! We must smurf this masquerade!

Oh! What's more-- you're right! With all these different medicines, nothing smurfs like before!

35

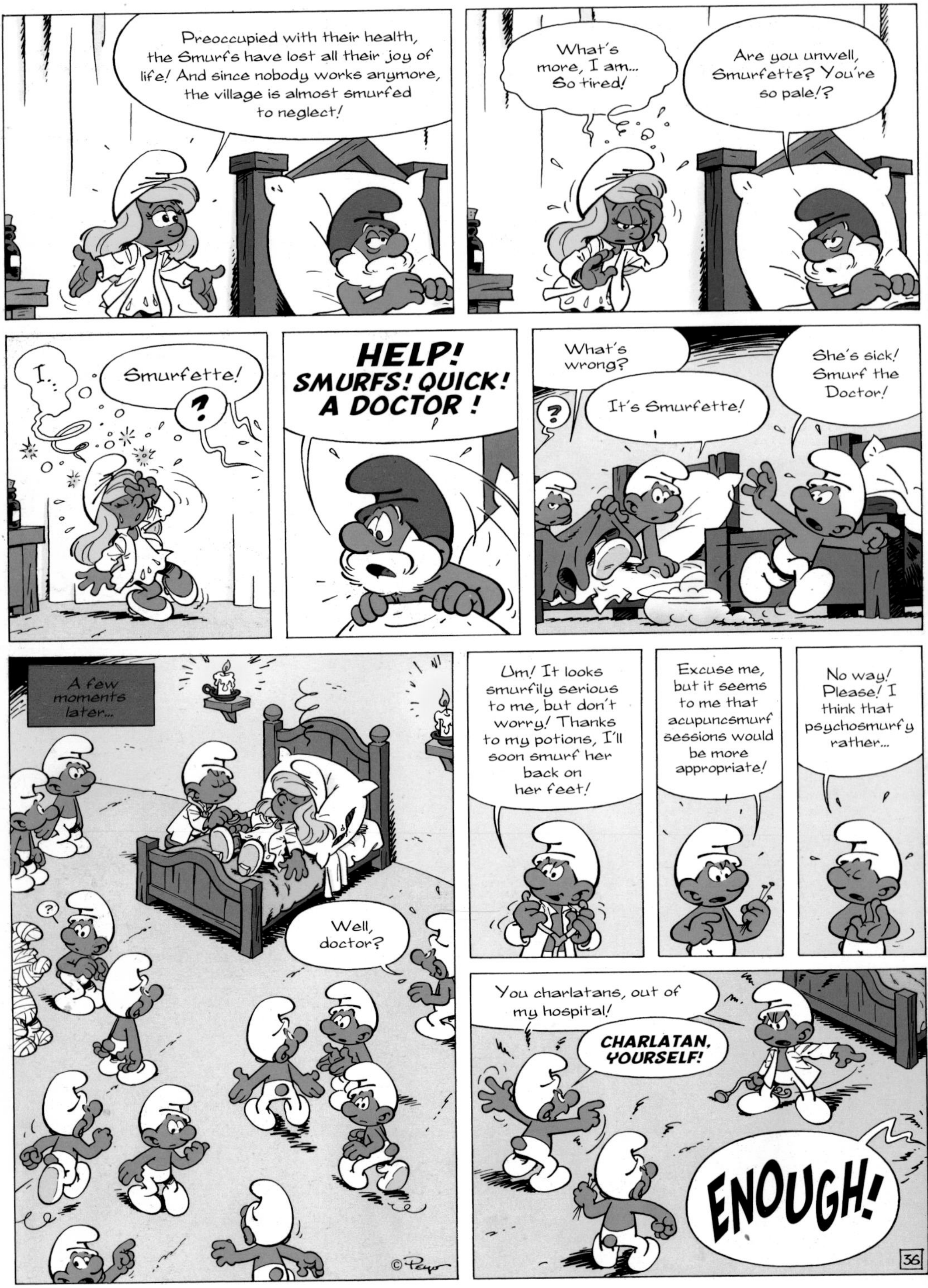

Preoccupied with their health, the Smurfs have lost all their joy of life! And since nobody works anymore, the village is almost smurfed to neglect!
What's more, I am... So tired!
Are you unwell, Smurfette? You're so pale!?
I...
Smurfette!
?
HELP! SMURFS! QUICK! A DOCTOR!
What's wrong?
?
It's Smurfette!
She's sick! Smurf the Doctor!
A few moments later...
Well, doctor?
?
Um! It looks smurfily serious to me, but don't worry! Thanks to my potions, I'll soon smurf her back on her feet!
Excuse me, but it seems to me that acupuncsmurf sessions would be more appropriate!
No way! Please! I think that psychosmurfy rather...
You charlatans, out of my hospital!
CHARLATAN, YOURSELF!
ENOUGH!
© Peyo
36

Aren't you ashamed of yourselves, fighting like this, when the situation is serious?!

Uh... Let's just say, Papa Smurf, that we're simply smurfing amongst ourselves about the best way to treat Smurfette! ...And we've finally reached an agreement!

She's in good hands!... Trust us, Papa Smurf!

I'm obliged to, since I'm too weak to smurf anything at all! One can always hope, at least...

Unfortunately, Smurfette's condition only worsens by the day...

Well? How is she doing today?

Well, let's just say that, for the moment, our medicine hasn't smurfed the slightest effect on her, but be reassured, Papa Smurf, it will before long!

That said, if we can't smurf that she's doing better...

We can't really say she's doing any worse either!

For smurf's sake! If I don't smurf anything, we'll have a catasmurfre on our hands!

Smurf me back to my bed, Brainy Smurf!

You're going to go smurf Master Ludovic, a doctor friend of Homnibus, who lives at the edge of the forest...

You'll give him this note and guide him through the forest to here! Take Hefty Smurf with you!

I hope nothing happens to them, or we're all smurfed.

You can count on me, Papa Smurf!

37

Brainy Smurf and Hefty Smurf are quick to fly to the edge of the forest...

And shortly afterwards...

That must be Master Ludovic's cottage!

Master Ludovic! Master Ludovic!

Who's calling me?

Oh! By Hippocrates's beard! Some Smurfs!

Homnibus has often spoken of you to me! How is Papa Smurf?

He's ill and Smurfette is, too! He sent me to smurf you this note!

Hm... The situation is grave, but I think I can help you!

Come in! One moment to gather a few things, and I'll follow you to your village!

Oh, by the way! Let me introduce to you a colleague who came to consult me! His name is—

GARGAMEL!

You know him?

Hey! Where are you going?

SPLOOSH

Gargamel is a dirty smurf! He's always trying to capture us to smurf lots of experiments!

BLUB BLUB

Tincture of Iodine

What are they saying? Is that true?

Come now! Not at all!...

Let's be careful! That old geezer will bring down the ire of the entire guild upon me!

Uh... It's just, in fact, an old misunderstanding I'm striving to smooth out!

Really!

Good! Let's go, Smurfs! Lead me to your village!

?

Their village?!

Um... Excuse me, dear colleague. Would you allow me to accompany you, in order to benefit from your so very enrichening experience! Perhaps I could even assist you?

?

!

ELI

That's an excellent idea! I'm flattered!

Heh heh! That way I'll finally know the path that leads to the village of those cursed Smurfs!

NO!

Don't do that, Master Ludovic! Gargamel wants to go to our village only to smurf all the Smurfs there!

Come, come Let's notexaggerate! I'm sure Gargamel isn't such a bad fellow! Look at him!

39 © Peyo

Now, hurry up and guide me! Time's a-wasting!

Hee hee hee!

That's how, very much despite themselves, Hefty Smurf and Brainy Smurf guide their mortal enemy towards their village...

And a few hours later...

There they are! There they are! They're back with the doctor!

?

HELP!
Gargamel is with them! He's going to smurf us!

?

Don't be afraid, Smurf friends! Gargamel came to help me! Take me to the patients' bedside!

! ? ? !?

Shortly after...

This is where Papa Smurf is smurfing! Come in, please!

SCRATCH SCRATCH

!

It's not true!? Tell me I'm dreaming! All these Smurfs, here, within my grasp!

?

40 ©Peyo

Are you there, Papa Smurf? It's me, Master Ludovic! I came like you asked me!

?

Uh... Excuse Papa Smurf, dear colleague, but he's resting! I smurfed him some of my potion, because he felt feverish again! I don't understand, moreover, why he had you come!

?

What did you give him?

It won't be long, soon, all these Smurfs will be mine!

The same thing as to Smurfette! It's a potion of absinthe mixed with an infusion of four-leaf clover! It's my recipe!

WHAT?! ABSINTHE? DEFINITELY NOT!

Ah! You see? I'd smurfed you that only acupuncsmurf could cure them!

Not at all! Psychosmurfy still seems appropriate to me!

THAT'S ENOUGH! Have you gone completely mad or what?!

Don't you know that, to practice medicine, you must study for many long years, and that you don't administer just any remedy in any circumstance? Playing the sorcerer's apprentice like that is dangerous!

41

Okay! Bring me the patients so I can examine them! Where's my satchel?

Shortly after...

This doesn't seem too serious to me! I think I can get them on their feet soon!

Bring me these different ingredients, as well as a big pot!

SCRITCH SCRATCH

Later...

Two leaves of woodruff, a hawthorn flower, and an arnica root...

The temptation is too strong! All right, I'll grab one, without anyone noticing!

Do you agree with me, Gargamel? An arnica root is necessary in the present case...

Uh... Yes, yes! Indeed!

Maybe you could even add a few pinches of gentian powder...

Gentian powder? Why, that's an excellent idea, dear friend!

The remedy is finally ready...

Three drops for Smurfette and three drops for Papa Smurf! There! With this potion, they won't take long to regain consciousness!

42

In fact, a few moments later...

Where am I?

?

They're waking up!

YIPPEE! They're smurfed! Hurray for Master Ludovic!

Ahh! Master Ludovic! I'm very happy to see you!

GARGAMEL?!... BUT HOW?

Be reassured, Papa Smurf! Gargamel spontaneously offered to accompany me to assist me!

I don't smurf very much about all this, Master Ludovic! But, if you tell me everything is smurf, I believe you!

Soon, they have to part...

I'm sorry I can't stay longer, but I'm expected at a conference! In a few days, you'll have completely recovered, and it'll only be a bad memory...

And above all, don't play being sorcerer's apprentices anymore! Your health is something entirely too precious to be taken lightly like that!

And especially don't go anywhere! I'll be right back! HEH HEH HEH!

Those Smurfs! What extraordinary beings! Don't you think so?

Uh...Yes, yes! Of course!

Then, right at the big oak, then straight ahead, until the stinging nettle bushes...

Shortly afterward...

Goodbye, dear colleague! You helped me a lot!

Not at all!

Yes, yes!

HA! HA! HA! Finally free of that old geezer! I'll be able to crush those cursed Smurfs!

So, first, go around the elf rock...

This place is familiar to me! I mustn't be very far from the village!

There! It's there! Behind that bush! I'm sure of it!

AHAAA! Tremble, you scrawny, blue wormlings!

43

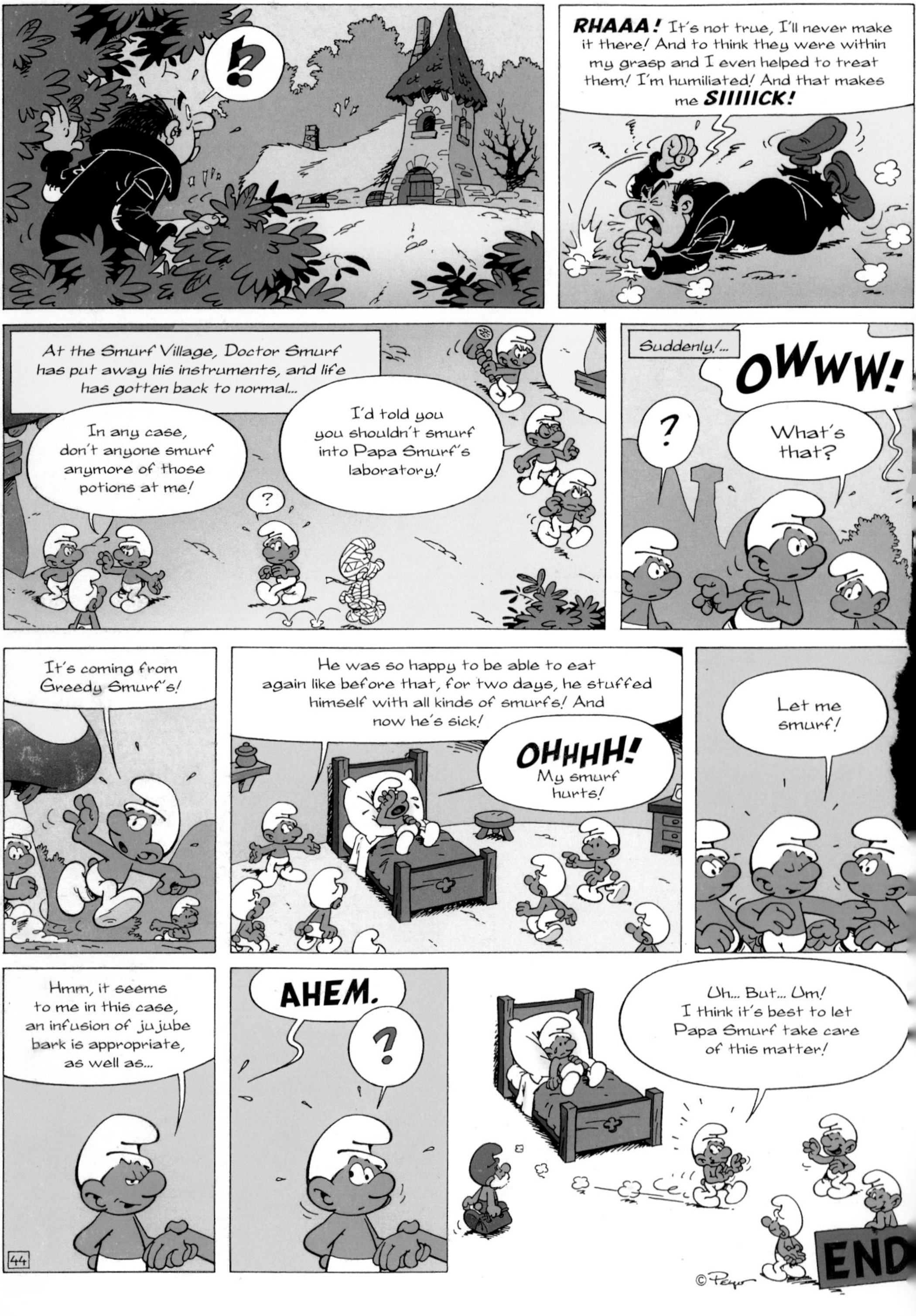
!?
RHAAA! It's not true, I'll never make it there! And to think they were within my grasp and I even helped to treat them! I'm humiliated! And that makes me SIIIIICK!
At the Smurf Village, Doctor Smurf has put away his instruments, and life has gotten back to normal...
In any case, don't anyone smurf anymore of those potions at me!
?
I'd told you you shouldn't smurf into Papa Smurf's laboratory!
Suddenly!...
OWWW!
?
What's that?
It's coming from Greedy Smurf's!
He was so happy to be able to eat again like before that, for two days, he stuffed himself with all kinds of smurfs! And now he's sick!
OHHHH! My smurf hurts!
Let me smurf!
Hmm, it seems to me in this case, an infusion of jujube bark is appropriate, as well as...
44
AHEM.
?
Uh... But... Um! I think it's best to let Papa Smurf take care of this matter!
END
© Peyo